MARVEL
STORYBOOK
COLLECTION

LOS ANGELES • NEW YORK

CONTENTS

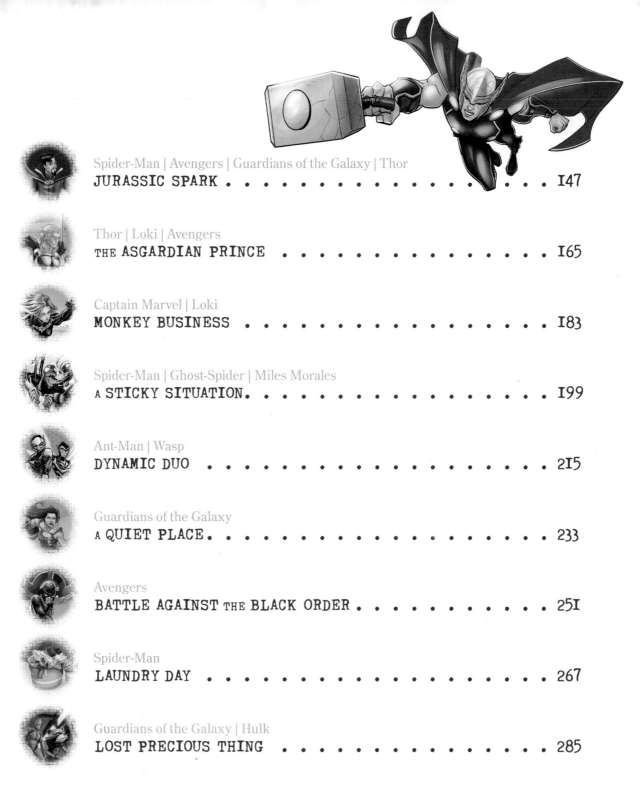

SUSTAINABLE FORESTRY INITIATIVE

Certified Sourcing

www.sfiprogram.org

SFI-00993

Logo Applies to Text Stock Only

SHORT
CIRCUIT

Peter Parker was at the movies with his best friends, Miles Morales and Gwen Stacy. Suddenly, the whole theater went pitch-black!

"Oh, man," groaned Miles. "They were just about to catch the bad guys."

An usher addressed the complaining crowd. "Sorry, folks," he said. "We're having a power outage. Must be due to the lightning storm outside."

Lightning storm? The three friends exchanged worried looks.

"Let's check it out," said Gwen.

Outside in Times Square, the

scene was frantic—someone had taken over all the city's power!

"My spider-sense is tingling," murmured Gwen.

Miles nodded. "Mine, too."

"That makes three of us," confirmed Peter. "One day I'd like my

spider-sense to point me to the nearest hot dog vendor."

The three heroes quickly ducked into an alley to change into their spider-costumes.

"It looks like Electro is up to his old tricks," said Peter. "He wants to use the city's electricity to strengthen his super-powers."

"We need to stop him before this becomes dangerous," said Gwen.

Suddenly, there was a loud *CRASH* as a truck collided with a car!

Following the pull of his spider-sense, Miles directed his attention to a strange sound nearby.

ZZZZZZZ!

Miles heard a loud buzzing and followed it down to the subway tunnels, only to find Electro! He was absorbing the energy from the subway rails.

Miles accidentally kicked a stray soda can, attracting Electro's attention.

"What's this?" Electro smirked. "Another Spider-Man?"

Thinking quickly, Miles fired a venom blast at
the Super Villain . . . and missed.

"You must still be in training." Electro laughed.

Angered, Miles tried again, this time with his web-shooters,
but Electro shot back with a lightning bolt that knocked him out cold.

"You better come with me, Mini-Spider," Electro said as he tossed Miles
over his shoulder.

Suddenly a familiar voice came from behind the Super Villain. "Electro, why so blue?"

THWIP!

Ghost-Spider fired her web-shooters, trying to capture Electro. *ZAP!* Electro blasted lightning bolts and knocked a stunned Ghost-Spider backward. Spider-Man leapt up onto the ceiling and tried to wrap a web around the limp Miles to pull the hero toward him.

WHOOOOOSH!

Just then, a train came thundering through the tunnel.

Spider-Man grabbed Ghost-Spider just in time. They clung to the wall as the train roared past. Once it was clear, they hopped down and looked around.

The train was gone. And so were Electro and Miles.

The web-slingers searched New York City, hoping to track down their friend and their not-so-friendly enemy.

Meanwhile, at the city's energy-control center, Electro had taken Miles and the facility's workers prisoner. He stood in front of a giant control panel.

"Once I hack into the system, I will be unstoppable!" Electro crowed.

"I think you've caused enough mischief for today," Spider-Man said as he burst into the room.

While Electro was distracted, Ghost-Spider crept in quietly and freed Miles. Before Electro knew what hit him, she swooped in and fired a pair of webs that pinned Electro against the wall.

But Electro quickly broke free. "MWAAHHHHHHH!" he roared, electricity coursing through him. Then he fired a supercharged lightning bolt that sent all three wall-crawlers ducking for cover.

"Miles," whispered Ghost-Spider, "your venom blast. It's the only way."

Miles was hesitant. What if he missed again?

"Don't worry," Spider-Man encouraged Miles. "We'll do this together."

Ghost-Spider quickly shot webs at Electro, while Spider-Man leapt into the air and tackled him to the ground.

"This place is crawling with bugs," hissed Electro.

"Now!" Ghost-Spider called to Miles.

Miles summoned his courage and fired his venom blast at Electro, shocking the Super Villain while he was fully charged. Immediately, Electro began to short-circuit.

With Electro in custody, the trio changed and headed back toward the theater.

"Thanks for having my back," Miles told his friends. "You guys showed me that being part of a team also helps you become great on your own."

"And you are a *really* important part of this team," said Gwen with a smile.

"Wow, my spider-sense is tingling," said Peter.

"Mine isn't—" began Miles, until he nearly ran into a hot dog cart. Miles laughed. "Movies, hot dogs, and catching bad guys. This is definitely the right team for me!"

THE WONDERS OF BLACK WIDOW

Natasha Romanoff, the Avenger known as Black Widow, was raised in Russia by a man named Ivan Petrovich, who took Natasha under his wing when she was orphaned as a child. Ivan trained Natasha in dance, acrobatics, and gymnastics.

"Da, Natasha," Ivan said. "Good."

She was the best of his students.

Soon, word of Ivan's extraordinary student got around. One day, several government intelligence agents came and took young Natasha away.

"Where are we going?" Natasha asked, more curious than frightened.

"Your destiny lies in the Black Widow program," one of them answered.

Now Natasha was scared.

The agents brought Natasha to the Red Room. There, she would train to become a secret agent. She wasn't alone—other girls were training there, too.

The Red Room conditioned Natasha to serve the government above all else. It became her mother, father, sister, and brother. She would defend it . . . with her life, if need be.

In the Red Room, Natasha became a fierce fighter—a warrior with few equals. She trained in aikido, judo, karate, and boxing.

After many years, Natasha earned the title of the Black Widow. Very few of the Red Room girls ever became Black Widows. It was a tremendous honor. Natasha was given a special uniform and two bracelets that fired "widow's bite" bolts that could take down superhumans. With her new weapons and her flawless training, Natasha would be nearly unstoppable.

"I will not fail," Natasha vowed. She knew her duty.

It was *all* she knew—all she was allowed to know.

Natasha
ran many successful
missions as a Black Widow.

She was always secret,
always dangerous.

But once she was away from her trainers, Natasha began to see that what she was doing was wrong. People were getting hurt because of her. She didn't like it . . . but she didn't know any other way.

Natasha encountered a hero called Hawkeye on some of her missions. He was her enemy. She knew that. And she fought him with all her strength, every time they met.

But there was something about him. Over time, his presence came to feel familiar—almost comforting. It got to where they didn't even *want* to fight each other anymore. Instead, Natasha preferred just to talk. He was one of the first people who had ever bothered to listen.

"You know, you'd think I'd know your name by now," Hawkeye said to her once. "My name's Clint Barton. What's yours?"

"Why would you ask me that?" Black Widow said suspiciously.

"Because you're a person," Clint replied, like it was obvious.

Black Widow didn't respond, because it wasn't at all obvious to her.

Hawkeye's question stuck with her. She'd been told for so long that her only purpose was as an agent, trained to serve.

Natasha didn't see Hawkeye for a while after that. But eventually, she was sent back to New York on a mission that could hurt many people.

She was hoping Hawkeye would find her . . . and he did.

"I don't want to do this anymore," she told him, feeling hopeless.

"I can help you," Hawkeye said. "Will you trust me?"

Natasha looked at his open, honest face.

"Yes," she said.

Natasha didn't know what would happen next. All she knew was that she was tired of serving the Red Room.

"I want to do good," she told Hawkeye. "I want to help people."

"I think I know just the person," Hawkeye answered.

Soon, they were both working for Nick Fury—and S.H.I.E.L.D.

And then, one day, a threat descended upon Earth.

Loki was coming.

"Black Widow, Hawkeye. I need you both," Nick Fury radioed over their comms. "This is going to take everything we've got. It's time to meet the others."

And suddenly, Natasha and Hawkeye were part of a team—a group of extraordinary people who had come together to defend Earth. . . .

The Avengers.

Natasha liked having a team. It was good to belong. But she never let herself forget the things she had done for the Red Room. She would always move faster, fight longer, and work harder to be better.

After all, she had a past to make up for.

BLACK PANTHER

VIBRANIUM CONUNDRUM

"Wakanda forever!"

T'Challa saluted the Dora Milaje as he exited his ship.

"Welcome home," his younger sister, Princess Shuri, said.

"How was the U.N. meeting?"

"I always enjoy meeting with other world leaders," T'Challa said. "But let's just say it is good to be back home."

"It is good you're back," Shuri replied. "There is trouble at the border."

T'Challa and Shuri joined Okoye and a group of Wakandan Border Tribe farmers in the palace throne room.

One by one, the farmers pulled up pictures of their land—sheep had gone missing, crops had been wiped away, and the farmers' construction vehicles had been destroyed!

"Help us, my king," the final farmer pleaded. "Whoever—or whatever—has infiltrated our border is destroying our land and our livelihood."

"If the border has been breached, we must find the culprit at once," T'Challa said urgently. "Okoye and I will investigate."

"I'm coming, too!" Shuri insisted.

"This is just a recon mission, Shuri," T'Challa explained. "To see what the threat might be."

Shuri smiled. "Exactly. If we find that the threat is out there, we need to protect what remains immediately." She lifted her hand and held up a high-tech ring. "What better protection than the portable Vibranium shield I invented?"

The trio headed out to survey the area, landing on a farm.

"These tracks look fresh," Black Panther noted.

"And the sheep are frightened," Shuri added. "We can't just leave them here."

Black Panther thought for a moment, then turned to Shuri. "We will take them with us." He pointed to her ring. "Under your Vibranium shield."

As Black Panther and Okoye followed the tracks through the farm and
into a forest, they found more of the missing sheep hiding. "You're safe
now," Black Panther said, directing each sheep on the path back toward
the shield.

Soon, they heard a faint noise ahead—a deep, guttural grunting.
Quickly, they hid behind some brush.

Suddenly, one of the branches started to crack. The creature cocked its head and locked eyes on Black Panther and Okoye, letting out a ferocious roar!

"It's a giant wild boar!" Okoye said.

"And it looks like we just interrupted his lunch—come on!"

Then Black Panther saw that the boar was headed straight for where Shuri was still standing under her shield.

"Shuri—watch out!" Black Panther called.

Shuri held firm—and so did the shield. "Mission accomplished," she said. "Now what?"

"We need to immobilize it," Okoye called.

"I have an idea," Black Panther said, looking back toward the farm where they'd come from, with its construction site. "Okoye," he began, "you're a fast runner, right?"

Okoye grinned, understanding what Black Panther had in mind. "Just try to keep up," she said.

The duo took off at full steam, leading the boar back toward the farm. "Now!" Black Panther shouted.

All at once, the two warriors stopped running and held their ground, while the boar continued charging. Just when he was nearly upon them, the duo leapt skillfully out of the way and the boar fell into a gigantic hole.

"Ah, the art of simple distraction," T'Challa said with a grin. "Not like your fancy technology, Sister, but it did the job, eh?"

Shuri rolled her eyes. "Lucky break," she muttered, then she clicked a button on her ring to deactivate the shield, but nothing happened. "Uh-oh," she said. "It's stuck!"

"Stand back," T'Challa called, getting a running start. He hurled a flying kick at the shield—but it didn't budge. "Sister, how do we pull the plug on this thing?"

Shuri's eyes lit up. "I know! The Vibranium is programmed to defend against attacks, but if you approach it slowly, it should recognize the tech in your suit and pair up."

Black Panther raised his hand slowly and rested it against the shield. "It's working—I can control it now!"

"I guess my tech still needs some work," Shuri said after she and the sheep had been freed, sounding a bit defeated.

"Princess," Okoye said kindly. "Your technology is wonderful. But sometimes it takes machine *and* human beings working together to be successful."

Shuri nodded. "You're right."

Then she brightened. "Well," she said, poking T'Challa, "I guess I will let *you* figure out how to get *that* back to where it belongs!"

GREAT SPACE
EXPECTATIONS

Since he could remember, Peter Quill had always wanted to know about his father. Peter's mother wouldn't tell him much for a long time—then finally, one day, she gave him a box of delicate trinkets and pictures.

"Peter," she said, "your dad was from outer space. We fell in love and had you. Your dad had to go back home, but he left a tracker you can use to contact him . . . if you ever get to space."

From that day, Peter dreamed of figuring out a way to get to outer space—and to his father.

Peter studied and practiced very hard, and after many years, he became an astronaut. He was finally ready to find his dad.

Peter blasted off into the cosmos! His tracker blipped and bleeped, growing bright. With every planet he visited, Peter searched for his dad. On one strange planet, Peter came across the Ravagers, space pirates who roamed the galaxy looking for treasure.

The Ravagers were taken by Peter's human appearance, and thought it would make him a good thief. They asked him to join them, and Peter agreed—on the condition they help him find his dad along the way.

The Ravagers were kind to Peter—they even gave him a brand-new ship, which he called the *Milano*. But despite the Ravagers' help, Peter still felt alone. All he wanted was to find his father.

One day the Ravagers stopped to refuel on Knowhere, a space station that resembled a skull.

Peter heard that an intergalactic emperor was visiting the planet. He saw the crowd of people cheering on the emperor, and couldn't believe his eyes. He pulled out an old photo he had taken with him from his special box and pushed his way forward to get a closer look. The emperor was a bit older and grayer, but the face was unmistakable: Peter had found his father!

Peter had so many questions!
He needs to see me, Peter thought.
He began to climb over the
protection barrier, inching his
way to the emperor.

"Hey! You're too close!"
Two royal guards yanked
Peter away. Peter cried
out for his father, but
it was no use. His
father could not
hear him.

Dejected and alone, Peter pondered his next move. He didn't want to return to Earth. Peter enjoyed traveling the cosmos, but not with the Ravagers, who only wanted to steal. Peter wanted to discover new things.

An idea struck: He'd travel the galaxy on great adventures, making a name for himself along the way. And maybe, just maybe, his dad would hear of this space adventurer known throughout the galaxy as . . . Star-Lord!

On his intergalactic travels, Star-Lord learned of a great warrior named Gamora.

As a young girl, Gamora had been taken in by the most feared Super Villain in the universe: Thanos! He raised Gamora and another girl, Nebula, to be dangerous warriors. While Nebula grew accustomed to violence, Gamora wanted to help others. She ran away from her evil family in search of something better.

Star-Lord tracked down Gamora, and the two bonded instantly. She understood Peter's quest to find his family . . . and his feelings of loneliness.

Before long, Star-Lord and Gamora
encountered a great warrior named
Drax the Destroyer.

Drax had lost his family long
ago, and traveled the galaxy
fighting against injustice, always
standing up for the weak. He
agreed to join Star-Lord and
Gamora, because he also
knew what it
felt like to be
without a family.
Drax would never
admit it, but he was
lonely, too.

The group's next stop was Planet X. Drax had told Star-Lord about the planet's sprawling forests filled with mythical treelike beings, and Star-Lord thought there might be an exciting discovery for him there. But the beings all shied away from the trio, except for one friendly tree named Groot. Groot's life on Planet X was pleasant but boring—he craved excitement and adventure, too! Groot asked to join the group on their journey, and Star-Lord welcomed him aboard!

The group's next stop was planet Halfworld, where they met a fierce-looking raccoon standing atop a pile of defeated aliens. But this was no ordinary raccoon. His name was Rocket, and a team of scientists had given him great intelligence! Star-Lord thought adding Rocket to the group, with his resourcefulness and smarts, would help them along their adventures, and Rocket was all alone—so he invited Rocket aboard their ship.

The team was now ready for greatness! But just as Star-Lord boarded their ship, his father's tracker began to blink! His dad was on planet Halfworld! Star-Lord and the group followed the tracker, and, when Star-Lord saw the emperor in the distance, he immediately recognized the emperor he'd seen so long ago on Knowhere. This time, he made sure his dad noticed him!

Star-Lord was happy he'd at last located his father, but he realized he'd already found exactly what he'd been searching for: a place that felt like home. And he'd found it with Gamora, Drax, Groot, and Rocket.

Star-Lord asked the group if they would stay with him and travel the galaxy together permanently, and everyone agreed.

The Guardians of the Galaxy were officially born!

SHOCK AND AWE

Peter Parker, the Super Hero known as Spider-Man, sat down on a rooftop's ledge after a night of fighting baddies. He let out a long sigh.

"Okay," said Gwen Stacy, Peter's friend and Super Hero partner known as Ghost-Spider. "Spill it. What's wrong?"

"Huh?" said Peter, confused. "Oh, sorry. I'm just tired. I haven't slept." He rubbed his forehead. "There've been these robberies, and I can't figure out who's doing them."

"Well, talk to me," Gwen said. "Maybe you just need a fresh set of eyes . . . I mean ears."

"Every night, a couple of technology targets are hit," Peter began. "Computer shops, tech start-ups, places like that."

"And at every location," he continued, "the security systems are shorted out. They're completely fried. I figured it was Electro, but I checked—he's behind bars."

Peter looked defeated. "So if it's not Electro, then who could it be?" he wondered aloud.

"That's odd! There've been a string of robberies in my neighborhood, too," Gwen said. "Homes, a grocery . . . even a toy store. But there's no sign of forced entry at any of them. I don't even know how the thief is getting in. When I tried to find out, the only thing I could find was some wet footprints. All the crime scenes had them."

"You know what?" said Peter. "I think I've got yours figured out."

"Then we've got that in common," Gwen said triumphantly. "Because I know who's robbing those electronics stores." The friends grinned.

Gwen and Peter put their heads together, working out detail after detail, idea after idea. They found that in using one another's strengths, they made a pretty good team! All they had to do was build the trap.

Or, in their case, a web.

The first thing they needed to do was find a target that would attract both criminals.

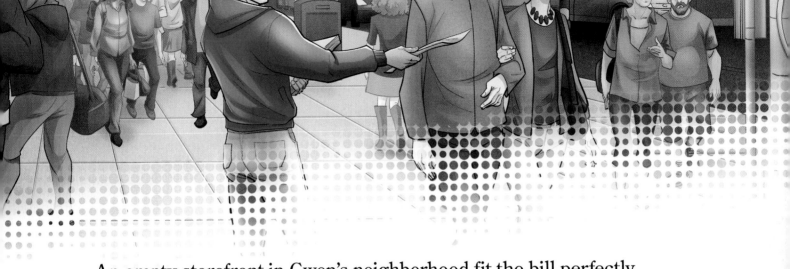

An empty storefront in Gwen's neighborhood fit the bill perfectly.

With a freshly printed banner and a foggy front window, they disguised the storefront as an up-and-coming electronics shop. Peter passed out flyers, and Gwen posted on all the top social media sites and tech blogs.

Their web had been spun.

Now it was just a matter of waiting for the sun to go down.

With everything in place, Spider-Man and Ghost-Spider perched on the rooftop of their fake store. They waited in silence, hoping to spot anything unusual.

"Yawn . . ."

Spider-Man was having trouble keeping his eyes open. But suddenly, his spider-sense jolted him wide-awake.

He scanned the street below and saw a thin stream of water making its way toward the building. It was as if the water was alive!

The water slid underneath the store's metal shutter. It moved a few feet into the dark room, then lifted itself up into the air. Slowly but surely, it took the shape of a person.

There stood the villain Spider-Man suspected had been ransacking Ghost-Spider's neighborhood: Hydro-Man!

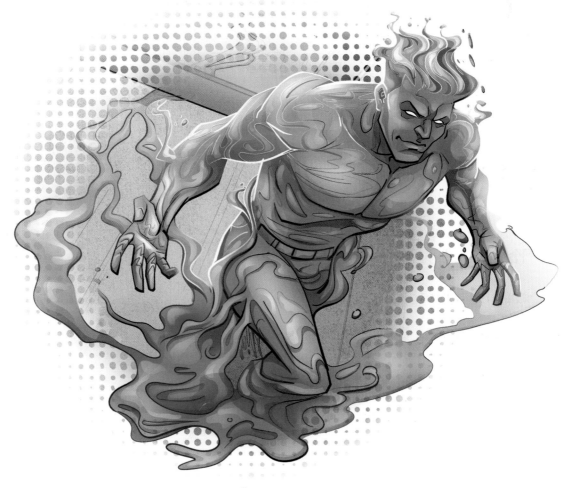

Meanwhile, Ghost-Spider spotted a shadowy figure approaching the back of the building. She ducked down low, keeping her gaze on the mysterious stranger.

Kkkkkzzzzzaaapppp! Electricity shot out of the figure's hands and into the automatic lock on the back door.

Ghost-Spider smiled beneath her mask. "I knew it," she whispered.

Her gaze met Spider-Man's and, with a nod, they took action.

Inside the store, the shadowy figure's hands began to glow. Spider-Man's suspicions had been correct: Electro *was* behind the rash of recent tech robberies.

Just not the Electro he'd thought.

There in the darkness was the newest electrically powered villain to plague New York City: Francine Frye.

The first thing Electro noticed was that this "store" wasn't much of a store at all. The second thing she noticed was a dark figure standing at the opposite end of the large room.

It's a trap, Electro thought. She immediately disengaged her electric charge. Now more than ever, she would need to stick to the shadows.

Across the store, Hydro-Man saw a spark of light out of the corner of his eye. He strained to see in the darkness. He could only make out a dark shadow standing by the open back door. Someone was waiting for him!

Hydro-Man clenched his fists. He was not one to give up without a fight.

The two villains bided their time for a beat. Then, at nearly the exact same moment, Hydro-Man lashed out with a blast of water while Electro shot a giant bolt of electricity from her hands!

FFZZZAAACRRRACCKKK!

Lightning met water in a tremendous explosion!

Sparks, smoke, and steam filled the room. Ghost-Spider took advantage of the chaos and leapt forward toward Electro, keeping her from causing further damage and mayhem.

Hydro-Man staggered backward. He had received such a shock to his system, he couldn't even think about turning into water at the moment. It was all he could do to try to keep his balance. Just then, Spider-Man leapt from the shadows.

"So this is what happens when you don't pay your water bill," he joked as he shot a web toward his opponent.

Hydro-Man hit the floor with a thud. He was down for the count.

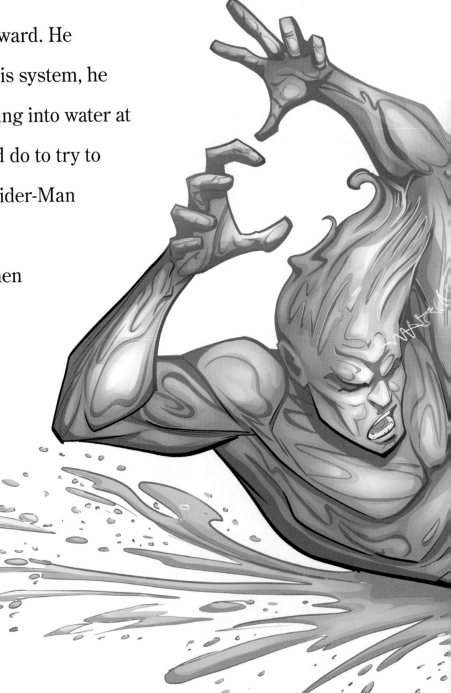

Later, back on the rooftop, the heroes watched as S.H.I.E.L.D. agents carted away the two villains.

"What did I tell you?" Gwen said happily. "A fresh perspective was all either of us needed. Now you can go home and finally get some rest!"

But Peter didn't answer. He had fallen asleep ten minutes ago.

ESCAPE FROM PLANET NIGHTMARE!

Captain Marvel landed on the strange purple planet. She'd been tracking a distress signal. Through the fog, she saw a green-skinned female warrior bearing a sword. Gamora! But what was the Guardians of the Galaxy warrior doing out here all alone? And who—or what—was she fighting?

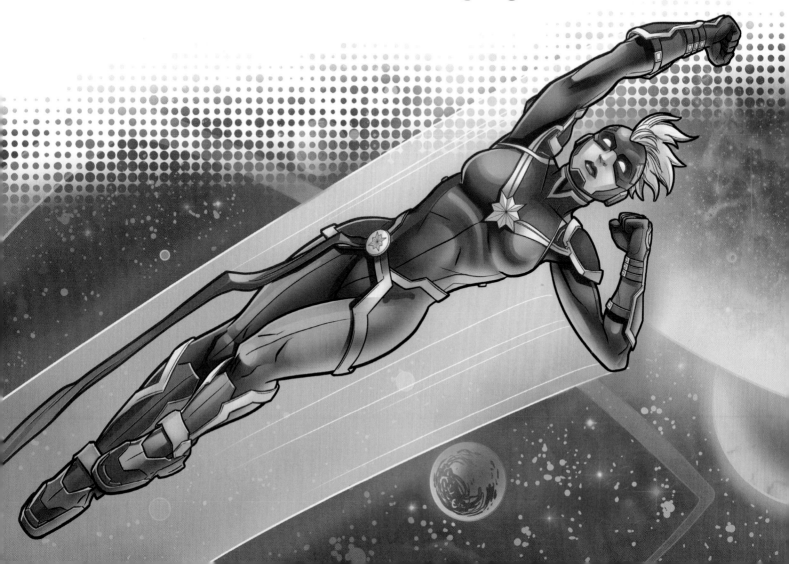

Suddenly, Gamora's opponent revealed himself—it was Thanos! "Oh boy," Captain Marvel muttered. She recognized the Super Villain immediately.

Up close, Gamora looked tired, like she'd been tussling with Thanos for hours. "Gamora, take a breather. I've got this," Captain Marvel said as she leapt to help Gamora, confident in her own power.

But just before Captain Marvel could reach Gamora and Thanos,

Yon-Rogg—one of her oldest enemies—tackled her from out of nowhere!

Captain Marvel gritted her teeth, momentarily caught off guard by the

alien's surprise attack. Thanos would have to wait.

"Captain Marvel! How did you get here? And where did that Kree come from?" Gamora asked as she continued to fend off Thanos.

Captain Marvel used her fists to blast her opponent with a powerful energy burst. "I intercepted your distress signal and came to help. As for this garbage heap"—she followed up her blast with a flying kick—"this is Yon-Rogg. Let's take these villains down!"

KA-POW! Captain Marvel's blast fired brightly.

SHWIIIING! Gamora's sword swung quickly.

But neither foe retreated!

"This is a nightmare," grumbled Captain Marvel, fighting off Yon-Rogg.

"Wait a minute—what if this place actually *is* Planet Nightmare?" said Gamora. "I bet that's where we are! It knows your worst fears and pits you against them." Her eyes widened. "That means these"—she gestured toward the offending villains—"aren't real!"

Captain Marvel's brow furrowed. "Real or not, how do we beat them?"

Gamora smirked. "We have to catch them off guard and give them something they won't see coming. Ready for a switch?"

The dynamic duo swapped enemies. Gamora challenged Yon-Rogg while Captain Marvel stepped up to Thanos!

"Let's get 'em!" Captain Marvel whooped.

Catching their adversaries by surprise, both Super Heroes quickly gained the upper hand.

But the villains were still a threat! Gamora landed a solid blow to Yon-Rogg, which stunned him for just seconds before he grabbed hold of her.

"That was a mistake, Kree slime," Gamora said through gritted teeth.

Thanos couldn't be counted out yet, either. He deployed his most dangerous weapon—his power-blast, which completely surrounded Captain Marvel!

"Are you okay?" Gamora called out to her ally. But there was only bright light and heat coming from where Captain Marvel had stood just a moment before.

"Better than ever." Gamora turned to see a super-charged Captain Marvel—apparently the Super Hero had absorbed all the energy of Thanos's power-blast!

"Grrraaaah!" Gamora twisted free from Yon-Rogg's grip and knocked him back with a right uppercut while Captain Marvel hurled a massive energy-blast toward Thanos that sent him sailing backward, out into the atmosphere.

"And that's how you do it," Captain Marvel declared, their enemies neutralized.

"Now let's hurry off this planet," Gamora said.

"It's been my worst . . . nightmare."

Captain Marvel prepared to leave Gamora's ship, just as the ship's incoming-message light started blinking. "Gamora! Gamora, come in!" Star-Lord's face filled the screen, looking worried. "Where have you been?"

Gamora waved at Captain Marvel as she flew off into space. "Oh, nowhere special," she answered Star-Lord. "Just making a great new friend!"

HULKING OUT

Bruce Banner wasn't always the Avenger known as the Hulk. Long ago, he was just a little boy in school, no different than many others. He was small for his age and was bullied by many of his larger classmates.

Unlike his body, Bruce's brain was very strong! He grew up reading everything he could about science, math, and chemistry. Bruce found teachers who believed in him and helped him become a scientist.

One day, Bruce made his most exciting discovery yet: He figured out how to use gamma radiation to cure the sick!

But General Ross had other plans for the gamma radiation.

General Ross commanded Bruce
to create a gamma bomb to help
the army in war!

Bruce didn't want to
make a bomb, but he felt
intimidated by Ross and
scared to say no. He
was being bullied once
again.

After months of
work, the bomb was set
up in a remote desert. The
team was about to detonate
the bomb as they watched from a
concrete bunker.

But suddenly . . .

. . . a truck pulled onto the bomb test site! Bruce saw a young driver, and shouted that someone had to go rescue him before the explosion erupted!

Bruce begged the army heroes who were at the site to try and save the boy. But the men just told him to go away.

Something stirred inside Bruce—a feeling he hadn't noticed before.

It was courage! It was an inner strength! Not muscle, but heart! Bruce was done being bullied.

Without another word, Bruce charged out into the bright desert!

But the countdown to detonation had already begun. . . . The bomb was going to go off!

Unaware of the danger, the boy had hopped out of his truck and jumped onto the hood, a harmonica in one hand.

The bomb was just seconds away from detonation when Bruce reached the boy. At the last moment, Bruce pushed him into the surrounding protective ditch, just as the bomb exploded!

But Bruce was caught in the gamma blast!

Ross and the army came out to inspect the bomb site. The smoke was thinning out, but there was no sign of Bruce or the boy, only the melted truck.

Just as they started to fear the worst, a giant shape appeared in the smoke, standing over the boy to protect him.

It was the Incredible Hulk!

The Hulk, thinking that the army might hurt the boy, defended him, snatching up tanks and tossing them aside. The army seemed like bullies, and the Hulk didn't like bullies. Even so, the Hulk wasn't trying to hurt anyone—he just wanted to keep the boy safe. But the army seemed scared Hulk would hurt them, and ran away from him.

After Hulk was sure that the boy was going to be okay, he flexed his powerful legs and jumped miles into the air, far away from everyone, feeling confused. What must he be, that people would fear him so?

Once Hulk was alone in the woods, he turned back into Bruce Banner. Bruce realized the gamma bomb's energy had made him strong, but that didn't make him happy—he was afraid he would lose control as Hulk and become a bully himself.

So Bruce decided he would walk away from his life and friends, and travel in search of a cure for what he thought was a monster inside of him.

Bruce Banner's journey would take him on many great adventures, and even though he would never believe it himself, he—and the Hulk—were both heroes with great courage and strength.

One day, the Hulk would even be an Avenger.

A TALE OF
TWO WIDOWS
PART I

High up in Avengers Tower, Nick Fury, head of S.H.I.E.L.D., was conducting his weekly briefing with the team.

Suddenly, Fury's comms lit up.

"Hmm," he said to the team, his face worried. "I've just gotten intel that Black Widow has been spotted in Russia. My sources think she's responsible for stealing some top-secret new technology."

The Avengers looked around at one another, surprised. Black Widow in Russia, committing crimes? Impossible!

Just then, Natasha Romanoff, the Black Widow, strolled into the briefing room, flanked by Hawkeye and Falcon. "Sorry we're late," she said breezily. "Training ran long."

She looked around at her friends' faces. She could tell immediately that something was off. Where there was usually animated chatter in the briefing room before the work began, the Avengers were quiet and solemn.

Her tone grew serious. "What's going on?" She waited nervously for them to answer. It was beginning to worry her.

The team reluctantly told Natasha there was a Black Widow spotted in Russia who was suspected of stealing cutting-edge tech, and that Fury was headed there to investigate the sightings.

"I'm going with you," Natasha said simply.

Being an Avenger meant a lot to Natasha.

She wasn't going to let an impostor ruin all of the hard work she'd done to overcome her past. Natasha sighed as she boarded the Quinjet a little while later. She didn't like Russia. But at least there would be blintzes there.

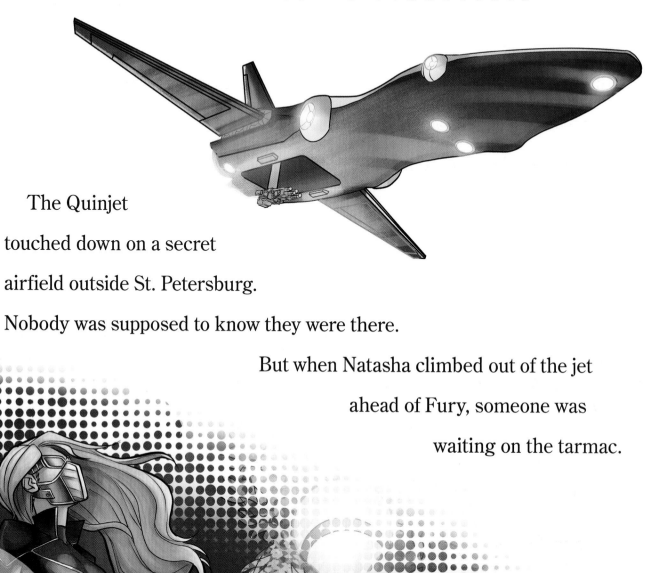

The Quinjet

touched down on a secret

airfield outside St. Petersburg.

Nobody was supposed to know they were there.

But when Natasha climbed out of the jet

ahead of Fury, someone was

waiting on the tarmac.

It was a figure wearing an exact replica of Natasha's Black Widow suit, her face covered with a mask.

"That must be you—I mean, uh, her," Fury said.

"Get back on your . . . paper airplane," the figure said, waving a disdainful hand at the Quinjet. "Go back to America."

"Who are you?" Fury demanded. He strode toward the figure. "How did you know we would be here?"

Natasha hung back, watching. Hearing the masked figure's voice gave Natasha a strange sense that she somehow knew this person.

A bank of fog rolled in and swirled around the impostor Black Widow.

"Leave," a disembodied voice said. "Now."

When the fog cleared, the impostor was gone.

Fury turned to Natasha. "I don't like this," he said.

Natasha didn't like it, either.

Natasha and Fury spent a few days investigating. Natasha got to eat some blintzes, which were as delicious as she'd remembered. But they didn't get any closer to finding out the identity of the figure in the Black Widow suit or locating the stolen tech.

Then, one night, on her way back to the S.H.I.E.L.D. safe house, Natasha heard a soft sound overhead.

Someone was standing on a rooftop above her.

It was the impostor!

"Get out," the masked figure said.

Natasha smiled pleasantly. "Make me," she replied.

The fake Black Widow sprang from the rooftop. Natasha ducked just as a boot swung through the air where her head had been. Whoever this was, she was fast—and good.

Natasha hissed angrily through her teeth.

Had she met her match?

Natasha threw punch after punch and kick after kick. Her opponent dodged them all easily. Finally, Natasha connected. *POW!*

The woman reeled.

Natasha was panting hard. While the woman recovered from her punch, Natasha grabbed her phone.

Beep! Her phone made a small tone. A distress signal was being sent to Fury.

Natasha slipped the phone back into her pocket and launched herself once more at her impostor.

A TALE OF
TWO WIDOWS
PART 2

"That was disturbing," Fury said to Natasha.

"Agreed," she answered. "Whoever that was, she fought like—" She took a deep breath. "Like me." More and more, Natasha couldn't shake the feeling that she knew whoever was behind that mask.

"They're sure that Black Widow is behind the missing tech," Tony told Natasha the next day. He sighed.

"This isn't a great look for the group, Nat," Steve added.

Natasha reeled. "I'm doing my best," she replied shortly.

"We know, Nat," Iron Man said, confused by her tone. "We didn't mean—"

But Natasha ended the call. She'd heard enough. She had to figure out who this person was and clear her name.

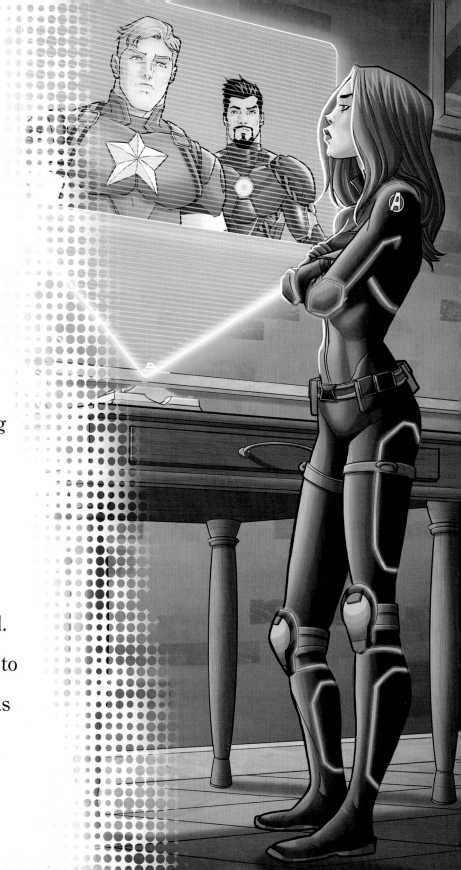

Suddenly, the door to her room burst open. Natasha leapt up—the other Black Widow was back.

"I told you to leave," the impostor grunted between blows.

Natasha threw her assailant into a huge mirror. *Crash!* It shattered.

They flew into battle.

At the last moment, Natasha reached out and grabbed the mask off the woman's face.

Natasha gasped.

"Yelena," Natasha said, shaken.

Yelena Belova had been like a little sister to Natasha back in the Red Room, where they both had been raised and trained.

Natasha had defected and joined the Avengers, but Yelena had stayed loyal to the Russian government.

And apparently she had been made a Black Widow, too.

"Yelena," Natasha began. "It's been so long—"

But Yelena didn't want to be friends. She wanted to fight.

"I have my orders," Yelena said coldly. Natasha dodged her blow.

Yelena kicked at her knee, and Natasha leapt into the air.

"Please—" Natasha started. But Yelena unleashed a sharp kick that caught Natasha off guard.

"Oof."

Natasha picked herself up. Now she was mad. She flew at Yelena, twisting under her swing to land a sharp blow to her ribs.

"Aah!" Yelena yelped. Natasha ran halfway up the wall and leapt backward, her feet aiming for Yelena's head.

But Yelena dodged just in time, throwing her momentum behind a kick.

The fight seemed to go on and on. Natasha wasn't used to working this hard. Usually she was the best fighter in the room. But Yelena was a Black Widow, too.

Finally, Natasha managed to pin Yelena.

"I'm not leaving," Natasha panted, "until you agree to come home with me." Now that she knew who this was, Natasha wanted to help Yelena—like she'd been helped so long ago.

Yelena's eyes looked almost sad.

"A Widow never fails," she said, quoting their motto in the Red Room.

Suddenly, Yelena twisted out of Natasha's grip and escaped. But as she disappeared, a small device fell out of her pocket.

Natasha picked it up.

It was the tech everyone had been looking for!

"Hurry back to New York, you two," Tony said over the video comms after Fury and Natasha had updated him. "I want to start analyzing that tech right away." He grinned at Natasha. "Great work, Nat. You make us look good."

Natasha smiled back. She should have known her teammates would never doubt her.

Later that night, Natasha and Fury were stepping onto the Quinjet. But before she boarded, Natasha stopped and looked out into the fog.

"Natasha," Fury said, putting a hand on her shoulder. "Let her go. You completed your mission." Natasha had told Fury what Yelena meant to her.

But Natasha understood that even though her mission was complete, this journey was far from over.

A Widow never fails. Natasha had a feeling Yelena had dropped the device on purpose. For Natasha.

Perhaps her little sister wasn't lost to her, after all.

Either way, Natasha knew she hadn't seen the last of Yelena Belova.

JURASSIC
SPARK

"**F**or Asgard!" cried Thor. A blast of lightning ripped through the sky toward his enemy Enchantress—who blocked it with an energy shield.

"Love to chat, but I have unfinished business on Earth," cooed the sorceress.

"Heimdall will not let you pass," Thor replied.

"Good thing I have my own way of getting around." With a snap of her fingers, Enchantress created an interdimensional portal and disappeared.

"Heimdall,

open the bridge!"

Thor had no idea how

Enchantress had escaped her

holding cell or what she planned

to do on Earth, but he knew he had to

stop her.

Enchantress was a powerful sorceress, and even Thor

was going to need some help.

It was time for the Avengers to assemble.

Nearby in the cosmos, the Guardians of the Galaxy received the transmission about Enchantress's escape.

"Hey, that's my home planet!" Star-Lord said. "Let's go help—and maybe pick up a hot dog while we're there."

"Why do we need a dog of any temperature?" Drax asked as Gamora rolled her eyes.

Back on Earth, Spider-Man swung toward a bright light coming from Central Park. *Whoa! It's too early for holiday lights,* he thought to himself. *Better check it out.*

Spider-Man arrived in the park to find

Enchantress reciting a spell, protected by an energy

shield around her. Thor hovered above and did not look happy.

"We can do this the easy way or the hard way," Thor said.

Just then, the Guardians' ship landed nearby. "It's over,

Enchantress," Thor declared. "You must surrender."

"You're too late," Enchantress said. "My time spell will make

me stronger than all of you."

"You need to fight magic with magic," a voice called out. Everyone turned to see Doctor Strange, who was working up his own sorcery. "Let's see how the sorceress fares when she gets a taste of her own medicine." He began to summon a portal.

"No!" Enchantress cried. "The spell cannot be interrupted, or else—"

Just as the portal descended upon her, Enchantress's energy shield splintered into thousands of fragments of blinding light. For a moment, the whole world seemed to disappear.

"Wait!" Drax called into the void. "Or else what?"

Seconds later, the three heroes found themselves in a strange field.

"Where are we?" asked Spider-Man.

Suddenly, an earth-shattering roar pierced the air.

"And what is that horrible noise?" asked Drax.

"Run!" cried Doctor Strange as a herd of velociraptors barreled down on them.

"Dinosaurs?" asked Spider-Man. "You have got to be kidding me!"

Doctor Strange used his magic to levitate Spider-Man and Drax out of the velociraptors' paths. But it soon became clear the dinosaurs hadn't been running toward the Super Heroes . . .

. . . rather, they had been running away from something else.

A giant T. rex, to be exact.

"Uh-oh," Spider-Man said.

"Help me!" called a voice.

"Looks like we aren't the only ones who ended up here," Spider-Man said, looking down.

Below them, trapped under a fallen tree, was the Enchantress.

"Quick," Doctor Strange said, setting Drax and Spidey back on the ground. "You two distract the T. rex. I'll handle her."

A pterodactyl flew by, giving Spider-Man an idea. He shot a web toward the pterodactyl, creating a lasso. "Grab on!" he called to Drax, and the two heroes were lifted off the ground, swinging side to side. The T. rex below them was mesmerized as its eyes tracked their movements.

Once Doctor Strange freed Enchantress from the tree, she turned to him, furious. "I was trying to find a powerful magical stone, but your interference caused my time-travel spell to backfire. We've all been sent back in time!"

"Then we will need it to backfire again to get us back to our own time. And quickly."

Enchantress summoned her powers and a beam of light began to grow around them. "Incoming!" Spider-Man called out as he and Drax came hurtling down from the sky. Just as the T. rex was about to bear down with one giant, clawed foot, the group disappeared with a *poof*!

"Gotcha!" Thor yelled back in the present, as the Enchantress fell right next to him. "You're coming to Asgard with me."

Thor peered at the unlikely group of heroes. "What happened to all of you?" he asked.

"Ah, that is quite the story, my friend," Doctor Strange replied.

"We'll tell you all about it when we have the *time*," Spider-Man joked. "Get it?"

"I get it," Drax said, his face stoic. "It's just not funny."

THE ASGARDIAN PRINCE

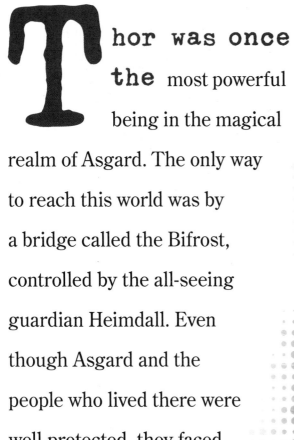

Thor was once the most powerful being in the magical realm of Asgard. The only way to reach this world was by a bridge called the Bifrost, controlled by the all-seeing guardian Heimdall. Even though Asgard and the people who lived there were well-protected, they faced endless threats from those who envied their wealth and power.

Thor was one of the land's great protectors.

Thor was born the son of Odin, Lord of the Asgardians, making Thor a prince. He and his brother, Loki, the adopted son of Odin, lived in a grand palace.

As children, Thor and Loki each wanted to prove their worth to their father. Eventually, Loki grew jealous of Thor because he was the favored son.

The throne was

Thor's by right.

To determine when Thor would be ready to rule, Odin had a special hammer made. It was forged from a mystical metal taken from the heart of a dying star. The hammer was named Mjolnir. It held great power. But only someone who proved to be worthy could lift the hammer Mjolnir!

Thor performed amazing acts of bravery and nobility, all while displaying great strength.

With every great achievement, Thor attempted once more to pick up Mjolnir. Just when it seemed like he would never be able to raise the hammer, one day Thor grasped Mjolnir and raised it high up into the air! Thor had proven himself worthy of his weapon, and he used it well.

Odin wanted
Thor to be a great
warrior, and he
had become one.
More important,
Odin knew Thor
had earned every
Asgardian's respect.
But Odin also knew
that Thor had begun
to let the power go
to his head. Odin
was not happy.

Thor was cursed
to live on Earth as a
mere mortal.

Odin made his son believe that he was a medical student with an injured leg named Don Blake. As Don, Thor learned to study hard, and in the end he earned his medical degree.

He allowed others to help him with his injury. In doing so, he learned to truly love humanity.

Then one day on vacation in Norway, Don discovered a strange walking stick inside a cave. When he struck the stick against the ground, it magically transformed. It was Mjolnir in disguise! Just like the walking stick, Don changed, too . . . he turned back into Thor!

Odin was pleased. His son had learned humility. He had become human in spirit, but still, now and forever, he was Thor.

As he fought Super Villains all over the world, Thor's presence attracted the attention of his brother, Loki, the trickster god of Asgard.

Loki had just the plan for defeating his pesky older brother.

On Earth, Loki coerced the Incredible Hulk into fits of rage in order to draw Thor into battle. But Thor realized what was happening and soon made friends of Hulk and the other Avengers.

When Thor realized that the Hulk had been manipulated by Loki, he knew he was going to need some help.

With the assistance of Iron Man, Hulk, Ant-Man, and Wasp, the heroes defeated Loki and forced him to confess his crimes. Thor knew he needed to continue to protect the people of Earth and Asgard from evil. And he couldn't do it alone.

So he partnered with the Avengers to tackle threats both earthly and otherwise. One important battle pitted the heroes against Fin Fang Foom, an ancient dragon who was set free and vowed to wreak havoc on New York City!

The Avengers, along with Elsa Bloodstone and Valkyrie, managed to get the dragon back to where he belonged. It was a hard-won victory for Earth's Mightiest Heroes!

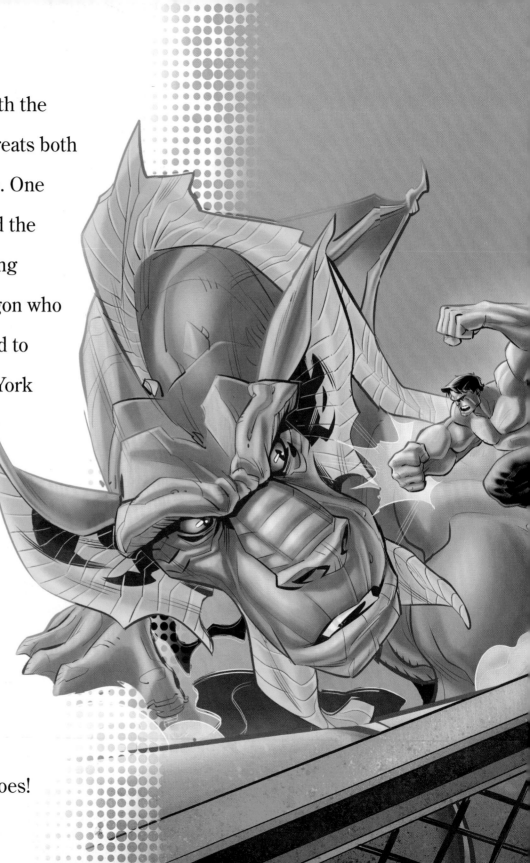

No matter the threat, Thor and the Avengers would make sure the people

MONKEY BUSINESS

On a bright, sunny day, Captain Marvel was flying over the New York City skyline when she felt her comms buzz. The Super Hero knew exactly who was radioing in.

"Danvers—you're late with the package!"

Nick Fury was not known for being patient. But before she could reassure Fury she would be at Avengers Tower soon, a voice cut through Carol's thoughts.

"Aaahh! Help me!"

Captain Marvel recognized the sound of distress all too well—in an instant, she changed course and flew toward the source of the cries.

Captain Marvel swooped in just in time to catch a little girl who was about to fall off the monkey bars.

"Well, that was a close one!" Captain Marvel exclaimed as she helped the girl to her feet.

"Thanks for saving me," the little girl said.

"She only had to save you because you're too scaredy-cat to finish the monkey bars!"

Captain Marvel looked around to see a group of kids poking fun at the little girl.

"It's not cool to make fun of someone for falling," Captain Marvel told the kids. "Everybody stumbles now and then." She helped lift the girl back onto the monkey bars' ladder. "Sometimes the bravest thing a person can do is get back up after they fall."

"Trust me, I may be a Super Hero and I may be strong, but I've been outsmarted before." She told the children about the harrowing past few days: the Asgardian trickster, Loki, had tried to steal a magical gem from a faraway planet. "He used the explosive rocks on the planet to attack me. I thought I had lost. But then, when Loki wasn't expecting it . . . I got back up."

"And you took something that I want back—now!" boomed a villainous voice.

Captain Marvel froze. She would recognize that voice anywhere.

"Loki! Show yourself!"

"Try right behind you!"

Captain Marvel turned around and couldn't believe what she saw. Right before her eyes, the little girl had disappeared in a swirl of smoke, and now swinging from the monkey bars was none other than Loki himself!

"Loki! It was you all along?"

"Yes—I am here to reclaim what's mine," Loki replied. "You may be strong, but your one disadvantage is that you are compelled to protect the weak."

Without warning, Loki raised his scepter and fired an energy beam.

"Run, kids!" Captain Marvel yelled, covering the children from Loki's attack.

The children ran in panic, but one of them tripped and fell to the ground.

"Nina!" her friends called after her.

Captain Marvel turned to make sure Nina was okay, and at that moment, Loki's blast hit her bag, and the gem popped out and went flying. Loki saw his opportunity as Captain Marvel ran to Nina. "Ha! Just as I predicted—you are a sucker for a damsel in distress!"

"It's okay, Captain Marvel," Nina said bravely.

"I may have fallen"—Nina quickly grabbed the gem and maneuvered back to her feet— "but I can always get back up!"

She threw the gem toward Captain Marvel, who caught it in midair as she leapt acrobatically after Loki, knocking him backward.

"Wow, that was so brave!" Captain Marvel said, after she had secured Loki and it was safe for the other kids to return.

Nina smiled shyly. "I remembered what you said about never staying down."

Captain Marvel's comms buzzed again. "I'm on my way, Fury—and I've got a two-for-one special for you today!"

A STICKY SITUATION

"**W**hat a great afternoon for a swing!"

Spider-Man flew over the skyscrapers of New York City, on his way to meet Miles Morales and Gwen Stacy for a training session.

After changing out of his suit, he joined Gwen and Miles at the Midtown High science lab.

"Hey, pals. What have we got?" Peter asked cheerfully.

"Just a sound cannon Miles is helping me work on," Gwen said. "I'm putting the final touches on it now."

"Awesome! But we better get going for our training exercises," Peter said.

"We've got to work hard if we want to be the best Super Hero team," Peter said, once they'd gotten to the roof.

"What should our team name be?" asked Gwen.

Peter laughed. "You're getting ahead of yourself. We need to learn how to work together before we have a team name."

"I want to show you guys something. I've been working on my bioelectric venom blasts," Miles said.

"Oh yeah? Throw a few of them my way," said Spider-Man.

FZZZT! FZZZT! FZZZT!

Spider-Man flipped through the air to avoid Miles.

"Your venom blasts are too wild and uncontrolled," Spider-Man called out. "Guess you need more training than I thought."

Gwen suddenly had a very odd feeling. "Guys, my spider-sense is tingling really bad," she said.

On the street below, long black tendrils appeared out of the sewers and tossed unsuspecting citizens into the air.

Miles spun a web that caught them before they hit the ground.

"What's happening, Spidey?" asked Gwen.

A burly black creature emerged from the spiraling tendrils. "Venom," growled Spider-Man.

"The alien symbiote that bonded itself to a human host named Eddie Brock!" Gwen exclaimed. "What's he doing here?"

"You don't really want to hurt people, Eddie!" Spider-Man called out. "How about we all calm down and go get some ice cream or something?"

"Eddie can't hear you, Ssssssspider-Man," the villain hissed.

"There's only Venom now."

"Then it looks like it's spider-time!" cheered Spider-Man.

Spider-Man flipped away from Venom's creeping tendrils. "Miles, might be time to put those bioelectric blasts to work," he called out.

Miles aimed his bioelectric venom blasts at the Super Villain while Ghost-Spider hurried to catch a piece of debris from falling onto a small group of tourists. "Welcome to New York City," she said, straining to balance the slab of concrete. "Sorry about the mess!"

"And now your friendly neighborhood web-head swings in for the grand finale," Spider-Man announced.

THWIP! THWIP! THWIP!

He shot gobs of sticky webbing in Venom's face. Spidey called to his friends, "That should keep him busy for a while.

"Man, that felt good," Spidey cheered. "I feel like celebrating. Who's up for ice cream? Unlimited sprinkles? Sounds good to—" *SWACK!*

Venom had escaped the webbing with ease and knocked Spider-Man out cold.

"Who's next?" Venom sneered.

Miles and Ghost-Spider pulled Spidey to safety. "I think I know how to take him down for good," she said to Miles. "But I'll need you to keep him distracted for a couple of minutes."

Miles spotted the brightly lit marquee hanging above Venom. He fired off a round of venom blasts at the marquee, causing a shower of sparks to rain down on Venom.

"Nice work. Be right back!" Ghost-Spider said, swinging away.

Gwen headed for Midtown High to retrieve her sound cannon.

She was ready to end the battle once and for all.

"Plug your ears," she said when she landed

next to Miles. "I'm about to turn things up."

VUUU! VUUU! VUUU! VUUU! VUUU! VUUU! VUUU!

Ghost-Spider unleashed the full power of the sound cannon on Venom as he struggled to preserve his monstrous form. "Make it sssssstop!" he screeched.

"Keep going!" exclaimed Miles.

Soon Venom's body reverted to a puddle of goo, revealing Eddie Brock's human form underneath. The police rushed onto the scene and took Eddie to jail.

"Gah!" Spider-Man exclaimed, waking up. "What happened?"

"Venom knocked you out," explained Miles. "Gwen flew in with her sound cannon for the save."

"Couldn't have done it without Miles running interference for me," Gwen said modestly.

Spider-Man felt bad about acting like he was better than his friends during training, when they'd been the ones to save him. "I was wrong earlier when I said all you've got to do is work hard," he said.

"A real hero also needs to work smart, like you did." He paused.

"Ready, *team*?"

Miles and Gwen cheered as the trio swung into the sky. "Ready!"

MARVEL

ANT-MAN

DYNAMIC DUO

Hank Pym was a brilliant scientist who had always been fascinated with the insect world, especially ants. Through his research, he discovered the Pym Particle. It had the power to shrink anything it touched!

That gave Hank an idea. Using the Pym Particle, he created a special suit. When Hank wore the suit, he could shrink down to the size of an ant. He could even speak to them! Eventually, Hank would assemble his very own ant army!

Hank could not only shrink and communicate with ants, but the suit also gave him ant strength! It gave Hank the power to carry, push, pull, and punch like he was his normal size even when he was small.

But villains began to hear about Hank's astonishing suit and wanted it for themselves. That wasn't going to fly with Hank! He began to use his suit to defeat evil. Just like that, Hank became known as the Super Hero Ant-Man!

For many years, Hank was both a scientist and a Super Hero. Spending hours in the lab during the day and being a hero at night made Hank tired. Hank's daughter, Hope van Dyne, knew her dad couldn't be Ant-Man forever. But the world needed an Ant-Man, and Hope knew just the person for the job— Scott Lang! Scott was an electronics expert whom Hank had taken under his wing.

After explaining her plan, Hope brought Scott back to her dad to tell him the good news. In the end, Hank agreed to Hope's plan. Ant-Man would live on through Scott.

But Scott was uneasy. He wasn't sure he could do it alone.

Hank smiled. Scott wouldn't be alone. Hank had been working on a suit for Hope, too. Finally, it was time. On that day, Scott Lang and Hope van Dyne became Ant-Man and the Wasp!

For months, Hope and Scott worked on making the Ant-Man and Wasp suits even better than before. Scott created a gadget that could grow and shrink objects. Hope created gauntlets that could deliver a powerful electric shock called her Wasp's Sting.

Then one day, Hope and Scott received a call from the Avengers! "We're facing a grave threat, and you two are the only ones who can help," Captain America said.

Scarlet Beetle, a longtime foe of the tiny heroes, was brainwashing bugs to create an all-powerful army!

They tracked Scarlet Beetle to his lair. "With the bugs of New York City behind me, I will become unstoppable!" he crowed.

"Not *all* the bugs," Wasp piped up. She turned to Ant-Man. "Let's take this bad beetle down a notch!"

It was an all-out insect war as Ant-Man and Wasp battled the Scarlet Beetle and his army of creepy-crawlies. The fight wore on, neither side managing to get the upper hand. Finally, they managed to best the Beetle. "Now bug off," Ant-Man said as he threw his shrinking discs toward Beetle, hitting his mark.

"Nooooo!" Beetle shouted as he rapidly shrunk back down to size. Ant-Man and Wasp cheered—they had won!

After winning the Battle of the Beetle, Ant-Man and Wasp joined the Avengers full-time. Whenever Earth was threatened, Iron Man, Hulk, Thor, Captain America, Black Widow, and Hawkeye would leap into action, but this time with Earth's tiniest heroes as a vital part of the team.

But no matter how much they enjoyed being part of a larger team, Ant-Man and Wasp were always strongest when working together!

A QUIET PLACE

"**A**nybody know what time it is?" asked Star-Lord.

"Not again!" groaned Rocket.

"This guy gets it," crowed Star-Lord. "It's mixtape time!"

"Peter, please," Gamora said.

"Make it stop!" shouted Drax. "I came here for sleep, not to shake whatever a 'groove thing' is."

"Yeah, Quill," added Rocket. "I'm tryin' ta concentrate here."

"I am Groot!" said Groot, dropping his playing cards in annoyance.

Peter had just found a new mixtape on one of the Guardians' missions. And while the others were trying to relax on this deserted asteroid, Star-Lord was too busy dancing to listen to them complain.

"Let's all just take a breath and—" Gamora was interrupted by a beeping noise from the *Milano.*

"Aw, great. The emergency beacon," grumbled Rocket. The group headed to their ship.

"Greetings, Guardians of the Galaxy," said an alien on their monitor. "The government of the planet Drakenthom would like to employ your services."

The alien explained that a band of intergalactic pirates was hiding out on

Drakenthom, a planet known for its complete silence, and that the Guardians

were needed to kick the pirates off Drakenthom for good.

"We'll do it!" Star-Lord agreed.

In no time, the Guardians had tracked down the pirates on a remote

Drakenthom beach.

"Put your hands where we can see them!" Star-Lord shouted as he

dropped from the Guardians' ship. He waved his blaster in his hand.

Gamora threw him an angry look.

"What?" Star-Lord asked.

Gamora didn't answer. She just put her finger to her lips.

It was just like Star-Lord to forget the only rule of their mission.

He mouthed, "Sorry." Then he studied the landscape, which was almost eerily quiet. For wanted criminals, these pirates were following Drakenthom's silence laws to the letter.

Before he could think too much about it, Star-Lord found himself leaping out of the way of a laser blast.

The pirates were firing at them just as the rest of the Guardians landed on the beach. Surprisingly, their laser fire was as silent as the pirates themselves.

The Guardians were overwhelmed. Star-Lord realized that without any leadership, the team was going to lose this fight, and quickly.

He was going to have to break the silence.

"Rocket, Groot! Take out the guns!" shouted Star-Lord. "Gamora! Drax! Force 'em back!"

The plan worked! But just as the Guardians trapped the pirates in one of

the beach's many caves, the ground began to rumble and shake.

A large dragon-like beast suddenly burst out of the caves.

And it didn't look happy.

"Ahh!!!" Star-Lord shouted as he ran for cover. The dragon followed him, shooting white-hot flames out of its mouth.

"Quill!" Gamora yelled.

The dragon turned its head toward her.

"The thing's attracted to sound," called Rocket as he, too, sought cover from the flames erupting from the beast's mouth. "And Captain Blabbermouth there woke it up!"

Drakenthom's need for complete silence suddenly made sense.

Without speaking, Gamora ran toward the Guardians' ship. She had an idea.

You like sound, buddy? she thought to herself as she reached the *Milano. I'll give you sound.*

Gamora was running out of time. But then her eye landed on exactly what she needed. Gamora grinned. *Bingo.*

Meanwhile, the dragon had cornered Star-Lord. It snapped its massive jaws at the hero and began to advance.

Then suddenly, it stopped.

Gamora had Star-Lord's boom box raised over her head, playing his new mixtape.

The Guardians took advantage of the dragon's distraction and rushed back into their ship. As the *Milano* took off, the strange beast followed close behind. It seemed that not only could the dragon survive in space, but he could also somehow hear the music in the Guardians' ship all the while. And he liked what he was hearing.

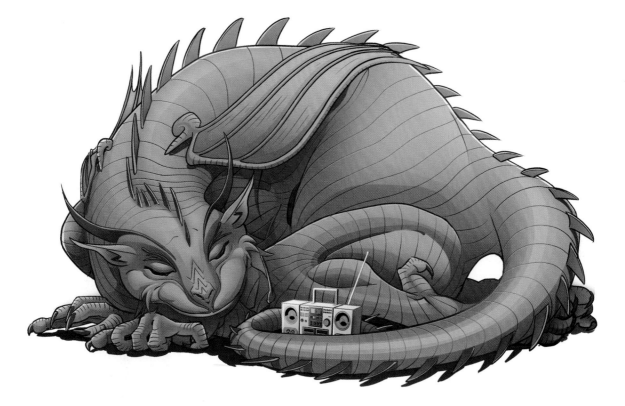

The Guardians led the dragon all the way back to the deserted asteroid where they had received the call from Drakenthom. Gamora descended from the *Milano* and gently placed the boom box in the center of a large crater.

As Gamora walked back to the *Milano*, Star-Lord looked longingly out the ship's window at the beast. It had curled around his boom box and fallen asleep!

The Guardians' ship flew off into deep space.

"I'm really gonna miss that tape," mumbled Quill.

Gamora looked at him sympathetically. But she didn't reply.

In fact, no one did.

No one was arguing. No one was even speaking. The Guardians of the
Galaxy were too busy enjoying some well-earned peace and quiet.

BATTLE AGAINST THE
BLACK ORDER

CRRAACK! A massive sound jolted Avengers Tower, where Shuri and T'Challa were showing Doctor Bruce Banner some Wakandan tech they were working on.

"What was that?" Shuri asked.

"It wasn't thunder, that's for sure," said Banner. "Let's check it out."

The heroes burst out onto the roof . . . and stopped in their tracks.

"Proxima Midnight!" Banner exclaimed. She was one of Thanos's strongest allies. "What is she doing here?"

"Give me a hand and I'll explain later!"
Captain Marvel called out, as she
fought the Super Villain.

Banner transformed himself into the Hulk and knocked Proxima Midnight right over the edge of the roof. But instead of falling, Proxima disappeared!

Back in Banner's lab, Captain Marvel explained what had happened. "Thanos sent two members of his Black Order to Earth: Proxima and Corvus Glaive," she said. "And now I've lost both of them."

Suddenly, a distress call came through. "Banner! Help!"

It was Ant-Man!

While Shuri stayed back to finish the tech, the rest of the heroes tracked the signal to the waterfront. "Boy, am I glad to see you guys!" Ant-Man exclaimed. "Who *is* this guy?"

Captain Marvel blasted the Super Villain. "Corvus Glaive. But what I don't know is why he's after you."

"Pym Particles," Corvus sneered, landing on his feet. The particles gave Ant-Man the ability to grow and shrink. "Thanos wants to . . . know how they work."

"Well, Thanos will not be finding that out today," Black Panther said firmly.

BAM!

Black Panther landed a surprise kick, bringing Corvus to his knees, at which point Captain Marvel discharged a knockout blow.

"That's what I call a one-two punch," she said, giving Black Panther a high five.

But just as Hulk was about to deliver the finishing touch . . . Proxima Midnight reappeared!

"Oh geez," Ant-Man said, shaking his head in disbelief. "There's another one?!"

"You were barely able to handle one of us," Proxima gloated. "How can you fight us both?"

"I was wondering that myself," Ant-Man said.

Without their whole team in place, they had their hands full!

How could the heroes stop them?

POW!

Shuri appeared and knocked Proxima flying with an energy punch from the updated gauntlets she had just completed.

With Shuri's tech, the Super Heroes quickly gained the upper hand.

"Better late than never!" Black Panther called out to his sister.

Shuri laughed. "The combination of Wakandan and Stark tech is unbeatable!"

"We've failed him, Corvus," Proxima called out to her ally. "Abort mission! I repeat, abort!"

Before the heroes could snag them, Proxima and Corvus teleported away.

"Whew," Ant-Man said. "That was too close."

"Piece of cake," Shuri said. "All we had to do was get the whole team together."

LAUNDRY DAY

BEEP BEEP BEEP BEEP BEEP!

"Gahhhhhh!" Peter Parker bolted upright from his bed and stumbled around his bedroom, still half-asleep, promptly crashing into his nightstand and landing in a heap on the floor.

When he'd gone to bed last night, he had set his phone to its loudest alarm. He wanted to be sure to wake up on time today.

The alarm had done its job a little too well.

"Peter?" said a groggy Aunt May from the doorway. "What was that crash?"

"Um, I guess I got up on the wrong side of the bed?"

"You and me both, kiddo." Aunt May smiled. "But now that I'm up, how about some wheatcakes?"

"Can't!" Peter exclaimed. "The big Tech Expo is about to start, and—"

"Whoa, cowboy," said Aunt May. "First you need to follow me." She led Peter downstairs and into the basement.

The room was a disaster. The Parkers' washing machine had been broken for weeks, and the laundry had slowly been piling up. Every day, Peter had promised to take it to the local laundromat, but something always got in the way. More often than not, Peter was too busy fighting crime as Spider-Man.

"You can go to the Expo when all this is finished," said Aunt May.

Peter didn't have time to argue. If he was going to make it to the Tech Expo, he'd have to get his laundry done as quickly as possible. Luckily, he knew the fastest way to get around Queens. . . .

As Spider-Man swung over the rooftops, his spider-sense tingled. The laundromat was just on the next block, right across the street from the Expo Center. Spider-Man scanned the area, but from his vantage point, he couldn't spot anything suspicious.

"Ugh, not him," Vulture said under his breath. The villain had spent weeks planning to rob the Expo's ticket booth. It would be easy pickings for a practiced scavenger.

Unless Spider-Man got in his way.

After a quick change in the back alley, Peter rushed into the laundromat. He threw his first load of clothes into the machine, then ran back outside again. He was just getting started.

Three hours, four loads of laundry, and way too much web-swinging later, and Spidey was finally finished. He swung back toward the Expo with his Peter Parker clothes in tow.

But just as Spidey reached the Tech Expo and got ready to change back to Peter Parker, his spider-sense went off like a siren.

Before he could react, Spider-Man felt himself fly upward into the air. The Vulture had grabbed him from behind!

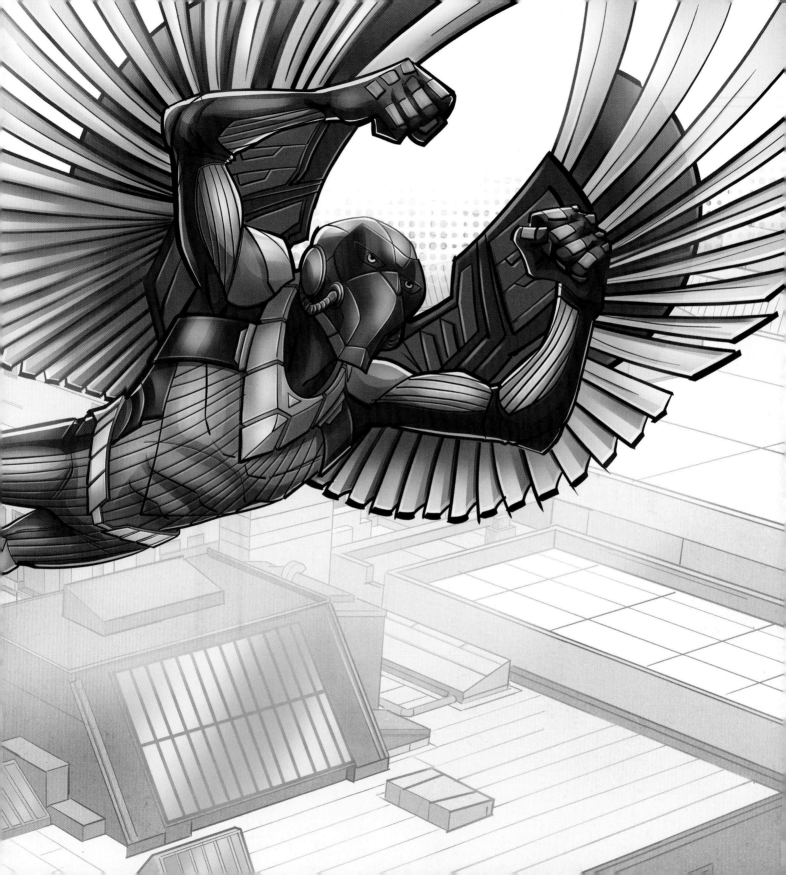

"Vulture?" Spider-Man said as they climbed farther and farther into the air. "Is this like an anti-Spider-Man thing, or just an anti-laundry thing? Because from the smell of your outfit—"

The Vulture didn't wait for Spider-Man to finish. He spun in a barrel roll. Spidey was thrown free!

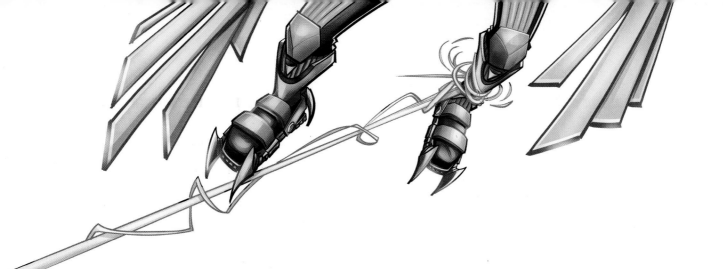

Spider-Man double-tapped his web-shooter. A thin line shot out and struck the Vulture's ankle. Then he pointed his other wrist toward a nearby building and shot out another line.

The Vulture tried to continue pulling Spider-Man upward, but the Super Hero held tight to his webs.

"Urghhhh!" Spidey gave the webs one final strong tug.

Vulture felt himself being yanked out of the air. He swung downward and crashed through the window of a nearby apartment building. Spidey swung down and stuck to the building's brick wall.

Spider-Man peeked inside. The Vulture was lying on the apartment's floor, unconscious. His Tech Expo raid certainly wasn't happening now.

Spider-Man returned to the rooftop to grab his Peter Parker gear. With the Vulture down for the count, it seemed the danger was over.

But his spider-sense didn't quite agree.

The building's water tower had been damaged during his fight with the

Vulture. Spidey turned just in time to catch the toppling tower as waves

of water cascaded over him. He gritted his teeth, holding the tower up

against the water's pressure.

Spider-Man set the empty water tower safely back on the rooftop. He still had time! One quick change, and he could finally go to the Tech Expo.

But when he found his clothes in the wreckage of the water tower, his heart sank. Everything was soaking wet!

Spider-Man's civilian clothes tumbled in the dryer as he gazed dejectedly at the emptying-out Tech Expo across the street.

He turned his attention to a woman snapping a picture of him with her phone. "Don't tell me you've never seen a Spider-Man do his laundry before," Spidey said.

She laughed. "Somebody got up on the wrong side of the bed today."

"Yeah," sighed Spider-Man. "You don't know the half of it."

"**Y**OU LOST WHAT?!**"** Peter Quill, also known as Star-Lord, shouted at Rocket, his small, furry, not-so-cuddly shipmate and fellow Guardian of the Galaxy. Rocket rolled his eyes. "It's called the Singularity Instigator. What do you care, Star-Bored? It's my stuff."

"We're the GUARDIANS of the Galaxy, not the ACCIDENTAL DESTROYERS of the Galaxy!" Quill shouted. "That thing can create black holes from radiation!"

"Don't get all wound up," groaned Rocket. "Look, I got a tracker on it. We'll have it back before you're done complaining."

In fact, Star-Lord wasn't done complaining, but when he turned to scold his raccoon-like teammate again, Rocket was on his way to Earth—and he'd taken Groot with him.

Rocket and Groot followed the tracker to a remote desert, where they ran right into none other than the Incredible Hulk!

"Oh, great," Rocket muttered. "It just haaaaad to be the Hulk."

"I am Groot!" Groot shouted, wrapping his branches around the green giant before Rocket even had time to think.

"Hey!" Hulk protested. "Off Hulk! OFF!"

With the Hulk all wrapped up, Rocket and Groot turned away to plan. But no sooner had they left the Hulk's side than he burst out of his restraints with ease! Rocket turned to Groot, frustrated. "We need an actual plan here!"

"I am Groot!"

"Well, okay," Rocket said. "I guess we *could* try talking to him first."

The duo cautiously approached Hulk.

"Why you tie Hulk up?" the green giant asked, more confused than angry.

"Because you took our Singularity Instigator!" Rocket shouted.

Now Hulk was even more confused. "Hulk does not know what fur alien talking about," he said. "Hulk busy looking for enemy."

"Well, we're lookin' for something, too," Rocket said. "Maybe we could help each other out." The Guardians filled the Avenger in on what had brought them to Earth.

After a few minutes of Rocket describing the Singularity Instigator, Hulk's eyes widened in recognition.

"Hulk see this garbage machine! Follow Hulk!"

Rocket grinned. "That's right, buddy. You help us, we'll help you track down this enemy of yours."

Rocket and Groot followed their new ally to a nearby ridge. Down in the crater, the Singularity Instigator was in fact there—in the hands of none other than the archenemy Hulk had been searching for: the Leader!

"Hey, Ginormous Head," Rocket called. "That's mine. What are you planning to do with it?"

The Leader smiled. "Why, I intend to hold the world hostage, or I'll create a black hole and destroy the whole planet, of course!"

Hulk grimaced. "Found enemy," he growled. "And dumb machine."

"Hulk, you got a cool battle cry or anything we can use?" Rocket asked.

"Yes," Hulk said as he lunged toward the Leader, yelling, "Hulk smash!"

The trio jumped into battle against the villain. Groot tried to grab the Leader, but his opponent had a hidden force-field generator that caused Groot's hands to splinter on impact. Rocket's rifle blasts bounced off the same powerful force field.

THOOM! The Hulk landed right behind the Leader. But the villain was ready for him with a powerful blaster pulse.

Rocket and Groot exchanged a look—it was up to them now.

"Groot, use our playbook—Cage Formation!" Rocket cried.

Groot's twiglike fingers began to extend longer and longer, branching off and twisting into a makeshift cage that encircled the villain. The Leader was so surprised, he didn't notice one of Groot's twigs was hiding an anti-gravity lifter . . .

. . . until Groot slapped the

device directly on the villain's giant forehead!

"Buh-bye!" Rocket waved as the Leader took to the skies, dropping the

Singularity Instigator on the ground in his wake.

"Hulk thanks friends," Hulk said as he hugged Rocket and Groot. "You helped Hulk fight enemy."

Rocket struggled to catch his breath. "And you helped us find our lost Singularity Instigator, Hulk. We'll be taking it back into space now."

"I am Groot," said Groot.

"Okay, okay," Rocket said, rolling his eyes, "we'll put it in a safe place this time. Somewhere no one will ever find it. Like Quill's underwear drawer. No one ever goes in there for anything anyway. . . ."